TRUNDLE

MR BOUNCER'S
HOUSE

FIRE
STATION

BLODGER'S
GATEHOUSE

SIGMUND SWAMP'S
HOUSE & BOATHOUSE

FERNYBANK FERRY

BROCK GRUFFY'S
SHOP

BRAMBLE'S FARM

CHURCH

VICARAGE

RAILWAY STATION

P.C. HOPPIT'S
HOUSE

POLICE
STATION

DR. BUSHY'S
HOUSE

N

W E

S

This book belongs to:

....

THE MYSTERIOUS FORTUNE TELLERS

Written and Illustrated by John Patience

PUBLISHED BY PETER HADDOCK LIMITED, BRIDLINGTON, ENGLAND.
© FERN HOLLOW PRODUCTIONS LIMITED
PRINTED IN BELGIUM
ISBN 0-7105-0678-3

The day before the village fête was all hustle and bustle. The Fern Hollow animals were busy preparing their entries for the various competitions. Mrs Tuttleebee and her daughter, Heather, were baking a blackberry pie.

Brock Gruffy was
tending his marrow

and Spike Willowbank was putting the finishing
touches to his painting.

The morning of the fête was bright and clear and everyone was bubbling over with excitement. There were stalls selling all kinds of things. The refreshment tent had been put up and Farmer Bramble was taking children for rides on Hazel, the donkey. But the thing that aroused the most interest was the funny, little tent in the far corner of the field and the peculiar person standing at its entrance. He had a big, black beard and wore a turban and baggy trousers. "Come and have your fortune told by the Gypsy!" he cried. "The world-famous fortune-teller will gaze into her crystal bàll and foretell your future." "I'll give it a try," said Brock Gruffy.

Brock was ushered into the dimly-lit tent where the mysterious gypsy sat hunched over her crystal ball. She wore a big hood and it was difficult to see her face. "Ah, I see you are a shop keeper," she said. Her voice was surprisingly deep. "How on earth did you know that?" gasped Brock. The gypsy began to chant:

"Your Past and Future I can see,
Everything that's yet to be.
The fortune-teller sees it all
Swirling in the crystal ball.
Cross my palm with silver, please."

Brock handed her a silver coin and was delighted to be told that he was certain to win the vegetable competition.

The fortune-teller was very popular. All the animals went to see her. She began each time by telling them something about themselves that someone from a land far away could not possibly have known without a crystal ball. Then she went on to tell them their futures. The gypsy's money jar was soon full to the brim.

"I think we'd best be off now before we're rumbled," growled the fortune-teller. She threw back her hood and revealed herself to be that rascally weasel, Snitch. "You're right," chuckled her assistant who was, of course, Snatch. "This false beard is beginning to tickle anyway!"

Outside, in the sunshine, Lord Trundle was judging the vegetable competition. "After due consideration," he said, "the first prize for the best vegetable goes to Mr Prickles's cauliflower." "That can't be right. The fortune-teller said my marrow would win!" cried Brock Gruffy. "She told me my turnip would win," complained Grandpa Bouncer. "She's a fraud!" exclaimed Mr Periwinkle. "She told all of us we would win!"

When it came to the painting competition, Spike was very upset to find that his painting only came second. "But the fortune-teller said that I would win," he sobbed.

Things were getting rather uncomfortable for Lord Trundle. He hurried off to the baking competition. "The first prize for the best cake goes to Mrs Bouncer's carrot cake," declared Lord Trundle. "That's outrageous!" exclaimed Mrs Tuttleebee. "The fortune-teller said I would win!" "Oh dear," sighed Lord Trundle. Meanwhile, Hazel, the donkey, was feeling a little peckish and, taking advantage of the confusion, she decided to help herself to Mrs Willowbank's jam sponge. Unfortunately she did not notice that the jam had attracted a number of wasps.

As she bit into the cake the angry wasps stung Hazel's nose! The poor donkey brayed loudly and rushed off through the fête with the wasps still buzzing around her head and Farmer Bramble chasing after her.

CRASH! Hazel plunged headlong into the fortune-tellers' tent. Snitch and Snatch were astonished. They were kicked by Hazel and stung by the wasps! Now everyone could see that it was Snitch and Snatch who had tricked them. "Well, they're getting exactly what they deserve," laughed Sigmund Swamp.

The two wicked weasels ran away, leaving the money behind them, and were not seen in Fern Hollow for a long time afterwards, and poor, old Hazel had some nice, cool lotion put on her nose. The money was given to Parson Dimly for repairs to the church roof which, as usual, needed doing.

It had been a fête to remember!

Fern Hollow

MR CHIPS'S HOUSE

MR WILLOWBANK'S
COBBLER'S SHOP

MR CROAKER'S WATERMILL

STRIPEY'S HOUSE

SCHOOL

THE JOLLY VOLE
HOTEL

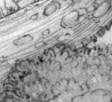

RIVER FERNY

MR ACORN'S
BAKERY

MR RUSTY'S HOUSE

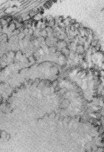

POST OFFICE

BORIS BLINKS'S
BOOKSHOP

MR PRICKLES'S HOUSE

MR TWINKLE'S
HOUSE

MR TUTTLEBEE'S
SHOP

MR THIMBLE'S
TAILORS SHOP

WINDYWOOD